CW01583050

The Snow White Lady

LIZ HEDGECOCK

WHITE
RHINO
BOOKS

Copyright © Liz Hedgecock 2016

All rights reserved. Apart from any use permitted under UK copyright law, no part of this publication may be reproduced, stored in a retrieval system, or transmitted, in any form or by any means, electronic, mechanical, photocopying, recording or otherwise, without the prior written permission of the copyright owner.

This is a work of fiction. While some of the persons, places and events may exist in real life, the versions presented here are fictional.

ISBN: 9781521993620

For fearless
vampire hunters
everywhere

I

Despite the weak autumn sunlight, there was a distinct nip in the air as I crossed Regent's Park. The cold wind found its way through my scarf, down my shirt-collar, and even up my trouser-legs, and I quickened my pace until I almost panted as I reached the steps of 221B Baker Street.

Mrs Hudson opened the door herself, and her face was wreathed in smiles at the sight of me. 'I'm so glad it's you, Dr Watson. Perhaps you can stir Mr Holmes to action.'

'Another one of his gloomy fits?' I asked, hanging up my hat and shrugging off my ulster.

'I'm afraid so, doctor. He needs a good case.'

'Well, as it happens, I may have the remedy right here.' I tapped my pocket and mounted the stairs, smiling to myself at Mrs Hudson's solicitude.

I found Sherlock Holmes lying on the sofa, his violin in his lap and his bow arm dangling.

‘Things must be bad if you can’t even be bothered to make a noise.’ I took a fingerful of tobacco from the Persian slipper and sank into the chair opposite.

‘What’s the point?’ said Holmes. ‘What’s the point of anything?’

‘To rid the streets of crime,’ I said, somewhat sententiously, as I filled my pipe.

‘Ha!’ snorted Holmes. ‘I catch one criminal, and another fills his place. So dull. And all the same; there’s no variety.’

‘No one said it was fun, Holmes.’

‘I just want a nice easy life. What’s wrong with that?’

It was my turn to snort. ‘Holmes, that is the last thing you want and you know it. Nothing would buck you up more than a juicy case. And I’ — I pulled an envelope from my pocket — ‘have just the thing.’

Holmes’s drooping eyelids snapped open. ‘What is it? Give it to me.’

‘I shall read it to you.’ I drew the letter from the envelope, perhaps a little more slowly than I needed to.

‘Come on, man!’ Holmes’s eyes glittered, and his long fingers twitched.

I unfolded the sheets and cleared my throat. ‘The letter is from an old school friend of mine.

We had lost touch, but — as your biographer I also have a certain notoriety.'

'Out with it!' cried Holmes.

I smiled to myself, and read aloud:

'Dear Watson,

Forgive me renewing our acquaintance in this way, with a plea for assistance. I am at my wits' end. I thought I had been tried enough, but no —

Excuse my disjointed scribbles, but I am beside myself. My only daughter died last month. She was ill for some time, and we knew the end must come soon. But it is not the end. She has been sighted walking abroad in the evenings — on the moor, in the village, in the churchyard! You will say this is fancy and superstition, a ghost, but it is worse than that. Witnesses say she has blood on her lips, and they have seen her pick up dogs and cats, bite them, and suck their blood. The villagers talk of the Snow-White Lady, and I fear my daughter has become — I can scarcely bring myself to write it — a vampire!

Watson, I can trust you. Please come down to Dartmoor and examine my daughter's body, so that I can set my mind at rest. And your friend, the celebrated Mr Holmes, if he cares to look into this… I am a rational man, not a fool, but the evidence is such to make me doubt every belief that I hold dear. Please wire me by return, and say you will come.

Yours in desperation,

William Holcombe, Esq.'

I looked over the top of the letter, expecting to see Holmes's eyes fixed on me, but he had vanished with his usual catlike stealth. From the bedroom I heard muffled muttering.

'Are you all right, Holmes?' I called.

Sherlock Holmes appeared in the doorway, a shirt in one hand and two neckties in the other. 'Am I all right?' He beamed. 'A death, a moor, a churchyard, and a vampire? Never better, Watson, never better!' His eyes narrowed. 'You've got a change of clothes in that bag, haven't you?'

I nodded.

'Then let us be off! Mrs Hudson, we have a case!' And the door of 221B banged behind us.

II

'Tell me something of your friend,' Holmes said, as the train rattled through the darkening countryside.

'There isn't much to tell,' I said. 'Well, there may be, but I do not know it. Bill Holcombe left school quite abruptly when I was fourteen. A distant relative died unexpectedly, and Holcombe's father inherited Mickleton Hall, in Devon. We said we would write to each other, but —' I spread my palms. 'Out of sight, out of mind, I suppose.'

'Quite so.' Holmes rubbed his hands. 'An ancestral hall, too? Oh, if I only had my index to hand!'

'You will see it soon enough,' I said. 'I wired Holcombe to say we were coming down tonight. From the tone of his letter, I imagine someone will meet us at the station.'

'But how will we find them?' frowned Holmes.

I glanced at the keen profile reflected in the

train window, framed with a deerstalker and caped overcoat, as was Holmes's wont for rural cases. 'I do not think we need to worry ourselves on that score.'

My intuition proved right. We had barely stepped from the train at Exeter St Davids when a strapping, tweed-suited man hurried towards us. 'Mr Holmes, sir? I am Mr Week, Mr Holcombe's land agent.' Never was a man less aptly named, I reflected as Week wrung first Holmes's, and then my hand. 'Mr Holcombe would have come himself, but — he does not like to be out after dark.' A shadow passed over his broad, ruddy face.

'I quite understand, Mr Week. I am sorry we have kept you waiting so long. I take it your gig is securely tethered now, and your horse calm.'

Mr Week first looked suspicious, then his chest heaved in a hearty laugh. 'You are every bit as good as they say, Mr Holmes.' He leaned in, conspiratorially. 'Go on, tell me how you did it.'

'I can tell you, Mr Week, but you will think it nothing more than a children's conjuring trick.' Holmes sighed. 'Very well. The mud splashes on your trousers indicate that you drove yourself, and their pattern — no higher than your calf — suggests a gig, as it has a high driver's seat.' Holmes opened his hand. 'Your handshake has left small traces of newsprint, yet you were not reading a paper when the train came in, suggesting you have finished and disposed of it while you waited. Finally, the cleft of your thumb shows a fresh red mark, similar to a rope burn. I conjectured that your horse had startled and required a firm hand to restrain it.'

Mr Week grinned. 'It does seem simple when you explain it.'

'Sometimes the simplest things seem most complicated,' said Holmes. 'I take it the servants do not know of my engagement, hence your journey.'

'The less they know, the less gossip they can spread,' said Mr Week. 'Let's get going. The last part of the journey is not best undertaken in pitch dark.'

The gig rattled along the well-made road at a clip. Holmes and I were furnished with travelling rugs against the evening air, and Holmes huddled in his with only the tip of his nose poking out. I wondered that he did not seek more information from Mr Week; but I did not care to tell Holmes his own business.

We turned left onto a narrower road, and continued about three more miles before turning again. 'Hold on,' called Mr Week from his platform. 'This is where it starts to get sticky.' I gripped my seat tightly, but Holmes remained as motionless as if he were carved in stone. Around us the trees formed a green tunnel, and the road seemed to blur even in the strong light of the gig-lamps. 'Misty,' shouted Mr Week. Droplets of water clung to us as the gig descended a steeper incline than any we had yet encountered, and the road began to twist and turn as it ascended. Perhaps the damp night air was getting to me, but I felt a distinct shiver pass down my spine, and drew my travel rug more closely around me.

The road curved, and the mist thickened until fat drops fell on us from the trees. 'Is it much further?' I called.

'Nearly there,' Mr Week responded. The road had narrowed to a single track, bordered by tall hedgerows; but I doubted very much that we would meet another carriage on such a night. Indeed, it felt as if we were the only people left on the face of the earth.

The road made a dog-leg, and ahead was a sparse show of lights. 'Mickleton village,' said Mr Week, nudging the horse to go faster. I saw cottages, a church, and some long shapes which I took to be farm buildings. We left the lights behind, and the road dipped sharply. I cried out involuntarily at the drop — and then we turned a sharp left, and in front of us appeared a well-lit stable yard.

'I hope you gentlemen won't mind waiting a bit while I put up the horse and cart,' said Mr Week. 'The stable-hands are long abed.'

Holmes jumped down from the gig. I followed, more slowly. I was stiff with cold, and my old war wound ached. We stood under the eaves for a few minutes, until Mr Week had stabled the horse. 'I'll settle her properly when I've taken you two inside,' he said. 'Could you walk on the grass? The gravel is rather noisy.' I wondered at the levels of secrecy attached to the operation of bringing us to the Hall. Nevertheless, we followed Mr Week's guidance, and squelched along in the wet grass, guided by his dark-lantern.

Ahead of us a wide, low building squatted against the dark grey sky. 'This way.' Mr Week cut across the grass and led us to a small porch where a candle had been left burning. The door's paint was peeling in long strips like tree-bark. Mr Week reached into his pocket and produced a large iron key, but before he could use it the door opened inwards, silently.

'Inside, quickly!' hissed a woman's voice. 'Have they come? Are they here?'

'Of course,' whispered Mr Week, and fitted himself through the narrow gap. Holmes followed him, and I went last.

The light inside, though not strong, was bright enough after the gloom outside to make me blink. I rubbed my eyes and saw rough-plastered walls, a coat of arms over a stone fireplace, ancient oak furniture, and a rich tapestry on the wall. Yet the interior, while striking, was nothing compared to the woman standing before us, clad in a black crepe dress. She was perhaps thirty, raven-haired, and beautiful.

'Good evening, gentlemen,' she said. 'I am Mrs Holcombe. My husband awaits you in his study.'

III

Mrs Holcombe put her finger to her lips and hurried us along a corridor hung with portraits. She tapped on a panelled oak door, and stood aside.

I had last seen Bill Holcombe at school. I remembered a tall, tentative lad, his frame not filled out. The man who looked up from the fire now was a stout country squire.

'Watson!' he exclaimed. 'You've barely changed.' He levered himself from his armchair, and shook my hand. I noted his florid face, and the dark shadows beneath his eyes.

'I know,' he said ruefully. 'I have changed — but it is this business. It makes my blood run cold to think of Amelia...' He shook himself like a terrier. 'This must be Mr Holmes. I won't say I'm delighted to meet you, given the circumstances, but I sincerely hope you can help me. Please forgive my plain speech, I hardly know what I am saying.'

‘It is quite all right, Mr Holcombe,’ said Holmes, shaking the proffered hand.

‘Nothing’s all right.’ Holcombe’s head bowed for a second. ‘But you must need refreshment after your journey. Mary!’ he called.

The study door opened and Mrs Holcombe peeped in. ‘Could you bring some food for the gentleman?’ He turned to us. ‘I am afraid it will be but a cold supper.’

Mrs Holcombe nodded, and withdrew.

‘Have both you gentlemen read my letter?’

‘We have,’ said Holmes. ‘Suppose you give us a little background, while Mrs Holcombe is engaged with supper.’

Holcombe gazed into the fire for a long moment. ‘There isn’t much more to tell. Amelia was the daughter of my first marriage — the first Mrs Holcombe died five years ago. She was just eleven, a bright, quick little thing, full of fun and laughter. Amelia was always delicate, and as she became a young woman it taxed her strength. You remember what a beanpole I was, Watson? Amelia was the same. She shot up, but for every inch she gained in height, she grew paler and paler. Our family physician, Dr Maloney, practically lived here, but no prescription, regimen, or tonic seemed to bring the roses back to her cheeks.’ He jumped up, and jabbed at the fire with the poker. 'I apologise, gentlemen,' he said, and bit his lip. 'I am no storyteller.'

'Go on,' I said gently.

Holcombe composed himself. 'I will,' he declared. 'Amelia loved her mother dearly, and was devastated at her loss. She turned in on herself, and became wilful. I couldn't manage my headstrong girl, and she taxed her governess so much that the woman gave notice. I advertised, and was lucky to engage an exceptional candidate, with impeccable references. Amelia took to Miss Lanchester at once, and, I must admit, so did I. Our discussions of Amelia's progress grew into intimacy, and I asked Miss Lanchester to become my wife.'

'The second Mrs Holcombe?' I glanced towards the door.

'Yes. We have been married for three years now.' He sighed. 'She is so kind, so patient . . .'

'Perhaps you could continue with the narrative, before supper arrives,' Holmes prompted, gently.

'Yes. Yes.' Holcombe mopped his brow with a handkerchief. 'Amelia seemed happier, more docile — though still not strong. I hoped she was getting over her growing sickness, although she still had a cough which concerned me, living as we do in this damp climate. I kept Dr Maloney close, and all seemed to be improving. Mary still gave Amelia her lessons, and seemed unconcerned. Then one day I came into the schoolroom. Amelia was alone, and stood to greet me. But confusion came over her face, and she sank back down. The poor child was unwell, and she had kept it from me — from all of us — because she did not want us to worry.'

'From that day I had no peace. Amelia ceased her lessons, and took to her bed. She said she had caught a chill walking on the moor — that cursed moor! We should have moved away when her mother became ill, but foolish pride stopped me. And this was the result, a poor innocent child doubled up in pain, coughing and retching and shivering. Mary stayed with her till all hours — I could not watch the poor girl suffer. But at least the end was merciful. Mary found her one morning lying in her bed, her cheek pillowed on her hand, as calm and peaceful as if she were asleep. She brought me to her, and you would not have known the child was ill. Her cheeks were rosy again, and — oh!' Holcombe choked a sob with his handkerchief. He put his head in his hands, and his shoulders shook. Holmes and I exchanged glances, and waited in silence for him to recover himself. At length he wiped his eyes, and sat back.

'I knew nothing of the — trouble — until a

week after we had laid the poor dear girl to rest. I was off to the village to speak to a tenant, when Week drew me aside, and said he would go instead. I protested — I like to feel I have a personal relationship with my tenants — and asked Week his reasons. He hummed and hawed for a while, but I dragged the truth out of him, bit by bit, about what the villagers said they had seen. I could not bear to confront them myself, but I saw, when I drove abroad on business, how they shrank from the sight of my carriage, and I knew —'

'What's that?' Holmes sprang up and strode to the window.

'Did you hear something?' Holcombe seemed dazed. 'No one should be there at this hour.'

Holmes paused, his hand on the crimson velvet, then drew it aside a fraction and peered through the chink. He stood motionless for some seconds before stepping away. 'I must have been mistaken. There is nothing to see.' He smiled. 'I think the lateness of the hour is preying on our minds. I propose we retire for the night and start afresh in the morning.'

Holcombe smiled wanly. 'That seems best.' Moments later a gentle tap sounded at the door, followed by Mrs Holcombe bearing a cold collation. Holmes and I made a quick meal, while

Holcombe himself took nothing, but watched us with sad, slow eyes. 'Mary will show you to your rooms,' he said. 'They are basic, but I hope adequate for your needs.' He passed a hand over his brow.

'I am sure they will be,' said Holmes. 'Mr Holcombe, do you take any form of sleeping-draught?'

'Not as a rule — Maloney has made something up for me, but I generally forget to take it.'

I stepped forward. 'As a fellow-physician, I feel you should take your doctor's advice. You don't look as if you have had a good sleep in weeks.'

'Perhaps you are right.' Holcombe stood. 'Yes, yes, I will do that.' He extinguished the lamps. 'The fire will burn itself out. Goodnight, gentlemen.'

Mrs Holcombe, candle in hand, showed us to our rooms, a pair of chambers tucked into a far corner of the house. I waited until her footsteps had died away before tapping on the connecting door.

Holmes opened it immediately, and raised his eyebrows.

'You saw her, didn't you?' Holmes's performance had been excellent, but to one who knew him as well as I did, the almost imperceptible set to Holmes's shoulders had given him away as clearly as if he had spoken aloud.

He nodded.

'What did you see?'

Holmes beckoned me in and motioned to the basket-chair, then took his seat on the bed. He spoke so low that I had to lean in to hear him. 'I heard a footstep on the gravel. I suspected a snooper, nothing more. But when I put my eye to the gap, she was standing at the edge of the lawn.' He pushed his hair back, and swallowed.

'What did you see, Holmes?' I whispered.

'A tall, slim young girl, her hair loose and flowing, dressed in a long white gown. She stood still, her arms at her sides. But her mouth and chin were smeared with blood, her dress spotted with it, and there was blood on her hands too.'

'Holmes, you don't believe —'

'She walks abroad, the letter said.' Two high spots of colour showed in Holmes's cheeks. 'The Snow-White Lady!'

I soothed Holmes, and procured a sleeping-draught from my own stock, but my mind raced as I retired to bed. Holmes was the least superstitious man I had ever met. For him to speak like this, he must have seen something uncanny. I got up to check the window catch and the door fastening several times before I drifted into an uneasy sleep.

IV

I had feared the gruesome sight Holmes had encountered the previous night would affect his health. However, he was up and about uncharacteristically early, and the faint humming from next door indicated that he was in a good mood. Presently a loud rap sounded on the connecting door, and I groaned.

'Come on, Watson!' cried a cheerful voice, followed by Holmes himself, fully-dressed. He sat on the edge of my bed and grinned at me.

I snatched off my nightcap. 'I take it my sleeping-draught worked,' I said, perhaps a little sourly.

'Like a charm, Watson.' Holmes's smile faded. 'I just hope Holcombe remembered to take his medicine, too. I suspect that if he had seen what I saw last night . . .'

'He is not strong,' I agreed.

'No. I plan to consult with the family physician today.'

'Dr Maloney?' I smiled. 'I imagine he is a good old country doctor.'

'Precisely,' said Holmes. 'It will be interesting to see you both examine the body.' I hid a shudder as he leapt up. 'I shall go and speak to Holcombe.'

He was forestalled by a tap on the door, and the soft voice of Mrs Holcombe. 'Gentlemen, when you are ready, breakfast is laid in the study.'

We sat down to bacon and eggs, and Mr Holcombe joined us. 'I have eaten already,' he said, waving away my offer of a plate. He looked tired, but less worn than he had the previous night.

'Mr Holcombe, I will get to the point.' Holmes laid down his knife and fork. 'You asked Watson here to examine your daughter, and that is the first thing we should do. I would also welcome a conversation with Dr Maloney on the subject of your daughter's health.'

'She was consumptive — she outgrew her strength —' Mr Holcombe stammered.

'I still wish to speak with Dr Maloney — in private, if I may.' Holmes's face was as impassive as a statue.

Holcombe went to the desk and scribbled a note. 'He'll come post-haste.' He rang the bell and stepped outside with the slip of paper, closing the study door firmly behind him.

'Why is our presence such a secret?' Holmes asked point-blank when Mr Holcombe returned.

Holcombe fiddled with a waistcoat button. 'I — well — the family . . .'

'Which is more important, your family or the truth?' snapped Holmes.

'It is not as simple as that!' Holcombe cried. 'The things I have heard — I want you to set my mind at rest, but I am afraid of what you might discover!'

'What do you think we might discover?' Holmes's voice was gentler, but his eyes were fixed on Holcombe like gimlets.

Holcombe stared at Holmes, his eyes wide. '*Ruin and dishonour*,' he whispered, and staggered from the room.

***

Holmes took advantage of our time alone to make an examination of the chilly study. 'The servants need a good talking-to,' he said, running his finger along the mantelpiece and inspecting the dust. Then he seized the poker and prodded at the ashes in the grate. 'They use far too much newspaper to light the fire, when they *do* bother to light it — wait! Watson, hold this.' He passed me the poker, grasped the basket-grate, and tried to move it, but he shifted it a mere fraction of an inch. 'The tongs, Watson! No, too big.' He leaned forward until his head was almost in the chimney, and stretched a long arm to the back, scrabbling under the grate. 'Got it!' He emerged triumphant, waving a tiny scrap of newspaper in a sooty hand.

'I hope it was worth the trouble,' I grinned.

'We shall see.' Holmes peered at the fragment. 'But I can tell you that this piece of newsprint was deliberately torn this small, and it is not from any common broadsheet.'

'A local paper,' I suggested.

'Possibly, but — I have seen this type before. Oh, to be in London, within reach of my papers!' He laid the scrap in his handkerchief. 'I shall wash my hands upstairs.'

In Holmes's absence I strolled round the room. Holmes was right about the servants' carelessness, I concluded, examining the crowded flypaper. Or perhaps Holcombe was an economical man. My hand strayed to the handle of the desk drawer just as a firm knock sounded at the door.

'Dr Maloney's here as you asked, sir. Shall I — oh!' A lad in an ill-fitting livery coat stared at me, and I daresay I returned the compliment. 'Beg pardon, sir, I didn't know Mr Holcombe had a visitor so early.' His prominent eyes ranged over me.

I assumed my best military manner. 'Show Dr Maloney in, please, then find Mr Holcombe and tell him the doctor has arrived.'

The boy raised his eyebrows at me. 'Right you are, sir.' He withdrew, and I heard an 'After *you*, sir' seconds before Holmes entered the study.

'I think our presence in the house has been noted,' I observed.

'Excellent,' said Holmes. 'I disapprove of sneaking around without good reason.'

The door opened, and Mr Holcombe entered, followed by a tall, thin, stooped man who reminded me rather of a heron. 'Dr Maloney, I presume,' said Holmes, extending a hand. 'I am Sherlock Holmes, the detective.'

Dr Maloney peered at him and nodded as he put a long white hand into Holmes's. 'Indeed, indeed. So this must be Dr Watson,' he said, turning to me and smiling even as he shook Holmes's hand. 'Always intrigued to read your cases, doctor. Although given how long the *Strand Magazine* takes to reach Devonshire, I daresay I am sadly behind-hand.'

'Shall we begin, Dr Maloney,' Holmes broke in. 'I take it Mr Holcombe has explained the reason for his summons.'

'Oh yes.' Dr Maloney's expression was grave. 'A bad, bad business . . .'

‘I have been invited to examine Amelia’s body,’ I interrupted, ‘and I would welcome your professional opinion.’

Dr Maloney looked at Mr Holcombe inquiringly. Holcombe nodded, and the doctor turned back to me. ‘Of course.’

Mr Holcombe walked to his desk and sat down. ‘If you will excuse me, gentlemen, I have some business to attend to.’ He opened the desk drawer and passed a ring with two large keys to Dr Maloney. ‘I shall await your return.’

Dr Maloney led the way through the house. ‘Miss Amelia is buried in the family’s mausoleum,’ he said, when we emerged outside. ‘It is a ten-minute walk from here.’

‘She died a month ago?’ asked Holmes, falling into step beside the doctor.

‘Yes, of consumption.’ Dr Maloney was halfway down the drive when he spoke again. ‘She rallied, and the family hoped for a recovery, but it was the final rally before the end. I tried to hint to Mr Holcombe, but he would have none of it. I am only relieved the shock did not kill him.’ He shook his head, and strode on.

The road was as narrow and steep as I recalled from the previous night, and I do not mind admitting I was short of breath when we arrived at the brow of the hill. The church tower loomed over the village, and I steeled myself for what was to come. A few villagers raised their hats to Dr Maloney, staring frankly at Holmes and myself.

'Are you privy to the village gossip, Dr Maloney?' I asked.

Dr Maloney's face hardened. 'I do not listen to such talk, and my housekeeper knows better than to repeat such things.' He stalked into the churchyard. 'That poor girl.'

The doctor walked towards a Greek temple in miniature, set at the corner of the churchyard. Its brooding presence shaded most of that side of the churchyard. The mausoleum was guarded by tall closely-wrought iron railings, but even through those I could see crude patterns scrawled on the stone in black paint.

'Your local wise woman has been at work,' Holmes observed. 'Those are ancient symbols, meant to keep the evil locked within,' he said to my expression of surprise. Dr Maloney unlocked the gate, tight-lipped, and we walked up the narrow path to the mausoleum. The second key slid into the lock of the iron-studded door, and turned with surprising ease.

Dr Maloney struck a match, picked up a lantern placed just inside the door, and lit the stub of candle. Then he closed the door with a clang. The lantern gave enough light to see rows of stone slabs set in the wall, carved with the names of the occupants. At the end a stone was missing, and the dark shape of a coffin stood in the niche.

Sherlock Holmes looked at Dr Maloney, who nodded.

'Why isn't she properly interred? Where is her headstone?'

Dr Maloney laughed. 'The local superstition is infecting you, Mr Holmes. The stonemason has broken his leg; I set it myself.' He led the way to the niche. 'Now, if you gentlemen will help me —' We put our shoulders to the job, and in slow increments we inched the coffin out of its niche and onto the stone floor.

Dr Maloney opened his Gladstone bag, and extracted a small crowbar. 'Not one of my usual tools,' he remarked.

'Wait,' said Holmes. 'Doctors, what do you expect to see when the lid is lifted?'

'I expect to see a decaying body,' Dr Maloney remarked, primly. 'Dr Watson, your view?'

I cleared my throat. 'I agree with my colleague. I expect a swollen, bloated corpse. The nails and teeth should have fallen out, the hair may have followed. The skin may well have blackened.'

'Would you care to do the honours, Dr Watson?' Dr Maloney proffered the crowbar.

I stepped back. 'After you.'

Dr Maloney inserted the crowbar into the seam between the lid and the coffin. 'Draw your handkerchiefs, gentlemen, I will not answer for the smell.' The wood groaned as it lifted, and the nails bent.

'Once more,' said Dr Maloney. This time the crowbar went in at a sharper angle, and the lid rose with a crack. We all jumped back as it slid half off.

Holmes was the first to approach, and we watched his eyes widen. 'My God,' he whispered. 'Look!'

Dr Maloney and I exchanged glances and stepped forward, prepared for we knew not what.

In the coffin lay a girl — no, a young woman. Her eyes were closed, and her cheeks flushed with a delicate pink. Her light brown hair cascaded over the shoulders of her simple white gown, and her hands were clasped in her lap.

'That is the girl I saw last night,' said Holmes. His voice had a crack in it. 'That is the Snow-White Lady.'

Dr Maloney clasped the girl's wrist for a few seconds. 'That is Amelia,' he said. 'And while she may look as if she is sleeping, she is stone dead.'

Holmes reached out and touched the girl's cheek. 'You are right. She is cold.' But as he gently put her hair aside, he moved with the caution of someone who does not want to disturb a sleeper. 'Did Amelia usually wear this locket?'

'Yes,' said Dr Maloney. 'It was her mother's, it has a lock of her hair inside.'

Holmes gazed at the locket for a moment, then lifted it from the girl's throat and peered beneath. 'Bring the lantern closer, Dr Maloney.'

The doctor obliged.

'Do you see?' Holmes pointed.

I gasped, and Dr Maloney cried out, as we saw the two little red puncture marks on the girl's white neck.

'It cannot be!' exclaimed Dr Maloney. 'There is no such thing as a vampire!'

'Normally I would be the first to agree with you, doctor,' said Holmes, and as he looked at Amelia's body his voice was as grim as I had ever heard it. 'But not today. Today I believe in vampires; and trust me, there is a vampire at work.'

V

'Holmes, what are you doing?' I half-ran by Sherlock Holmes's side in my attempt to keep up. 'What are we going to tell Holcombe?'

'Don't worry, Watson, I have a plan.' Holmes's face was set and stern as he strode down the hill.

'You're not going to tell him you think his daughter is a vampire, are you?' I panted.

Holmes stopped dead. 'Watson, do you take me for an idiot?' He glared at me for several seconds before stalking away.

'You might at least tell me your plan!' I shouted after him.

Holmes stopped again and waited for me. 'Watson, I am going to do what I should have done in the first place. I am going to run this case my way. Holcombe may be an old friend of yours, but he has been packed in cotton wool for too long.'

'Be careful, Holmes. Bill Holcombe is not a

well man.'

'I am aware of that. Now, let me take the lead.'

Our footsteps crunched the gravel drive. Holmes tugged the bell-pull, and the lad in livery reappeared. 'Yes?'

'Kindly tell Mrs Holcombe that we request a few minutes' conversation,' Holmes said, in his blandest voice.

The youth nodded, and left us on the doorstep. He reappeared a minute later. 'You'd better come in.'

We were shown into a small drawing room. Mrs Holcombe was sitting on a high-backed settee. A workbox stood next to her, and a hoop with a half-finished embroidery of poppies lay on her lap. She rose at our arrival, her dark eyes wide with alarm. 'I thought you would go straight to Mr Holcombe,' she quavered. 'Is it — is it bad news?'

'Mrs Holcombe, we judged it best to speak to you first, since your husband is not strong.' Holmes's voice had softened considerably. 'May we sit down?'

'Of course.' She indicated a seat. 'I apologise, I am forgetting my manners —'

'Not at all.' Holmes sat opposite her. 'I wish to ask you a few questions, if I may, about Amelia. I understand she was unwell for quite some time?'

‘That is correct. We hoped it was just growing pains, but as you know…’ Her voice faded, and she turned her head away as if in pain.

‘Do you think the damp climate here had anything to do with Amelia’s illness?’

A faint flush tinged Mrs Holcombe's pale cheeks. ‘Yes, I do. I suggested a few times that we should move somewhere with a better climate, but my husband would not hear of leaving the Hall. He is a fresh-air, windows-open sort of man.’

‘Did Amelia sleep with her window open?’ Holmes was almost on the edge of his seat.

‘She did — oh!’ Mrs Holcombe’s mouth made a little round O. ‘You think something got in!’

Holmes looked at the floor and wound his watch-chain round his finger. ‘I would not like to say either way,’ he admitted. ‘But if I could examine the room where she slept —’

Mrs Holcombe put a hand to her heart, and rose. ‘Of course. Oh, my poor dear girl!’

The graceful figure of Mrs Holcombe led the way to a pretty room papered in a cheerful apple-green, though the damp had caused a few peeling corners. I took in the furnishings — the little white bed, the dressing-table, the bookshelf — while Holmes examined the window-catch, and tried the window in various positions. ‘How far open was the window as a rule, Mrs Holcombe?'

'About so far.' She stepped forward and adjusted the latch.

'I see.' Holmes regarded the gap with narrowed eyes. 'The window faces the moors, I perceive.'

'Yes, Amelia loved the view.'

'She loved clothes, too,' I said, indicating the framed fashion-plates on the walls.

Mrs Holcombe broke into a delighted laugh. 'She did, Dr Watson! Amelia was becoming a young lady . . .' Her smile faded as quickly as it had come, and she dabbed at her eyes with a handkerchief.

'How did Amelia amuse herself, Mrs Holcombe? You mentioned that she loved the moors. Did she go for walks?'

'Not as much as she wanted, due to her weak chest,' sighed Mrs Holcombe. 'She read — novels, and poetry, and magazines — and sewed, and played the piano. Sometimes I accompanied her to a local dance.'

'Did she ever seem discontented?' asked Holmes.

'No, never.' Mrs Holcombe frowned. 'Why do you ask me that, Mr Holmes?'

'I am not quite sure,' said Holmes, slowly. 'I suppose I am trying to piece together Amelia's character. Would you say she was a strong character, or a weak one, Mrs Holcombe?'

Mrs Holcombe's arched eyebrows puckered in a tiny frown. 'I would say — not weak, Mr Holmes, but easily led, as young girls so often are. But we took good care to keep bad influences at bay. We did not expose her to village gossip and nonsense —'

'I am sure you did your best,' Mr Holmes leaned forward and patted Mrs Holcombe's arm. 'It must be very difficult to take the place of a mother.' Mrs Holcombe nodded, and I looked away. I could not bear to see her cry.

'Shall I ring for your maid, Mrs Holcombe?' Holmes asked.

'P-p-please…' She buried her face in her handkerchief.

'Come, Watson.' Holmes rose. 'Mrs Holcombe, we shall return for dinner, and that is when I shall break the news to your husband. Please can you shield him until then; the truth will be hard enough when it comes.'

She nodded, and we tiptoed from the room.

'What now, Holmes?' I asked, as the front door closed behind us.

'We are going to the inn, and I am going to have a drink.' Holmes set off up the road at a stiff pace, and I trotted after him.

As we walked into the inn someone stage-whispered 'It's the detective!', followed by an immediate buzz of conversation.

'Good news travels fast, I perceive,' said Holmes, walking to the bar. 'Two pints of ale, please, landlord.'

The publican finished wiping a glass and touched his forelock. 'On the house to you, sir. How's the vampire hunt going?'

'I think we're almost there,' remarked Holmes.

'Well, the sooner she's dealt with, the better. My poor old spaniel has never been the same since she got hold of him. He shivers every time a body goes near him, so he does. A nice sharp stake through the heart, that's the thing to do, sir. An' if you don't have a stake, I'll give you the run of my woodpile with pleasure.'

'That is a very kind offer.' Holmes took a pull at his beer.

'Least I can do, sir.' The innkeeper mopped at a puddle of liquid on the bar. 'We want people to feel they can walk home quiet-like at night, and not be huddling indoors in a quiver. And all over that flighty young piece.'

Holmes sipped at his beer again. 'Was she flighty? Her father said —'

'Her father didn't know the half of it! She'd walk down the street, nose in the air, tossing her curls at the young men, and you'd see her at the dances with her chest half-out. It's no wonder she caught a cold.'

'It was more than a cold —' I tried to interject, but the man was in full flow.

'And it ought to be too, the way she carried on! She used to be such a nice shy little thing, till the devil took her. That poor governess was no match for Miss Amelia in one of her moods.'

'Do you mean Mrs Holcombe?' asked Holmes.

'I do, begging her pardon. Now she *is* a lady.' The publican nodded with an air of finality, and wandered to the other side of the bar. 'Usual, Matt?' To my surprise I saw that he was addressing Mr Week. I raised a hand in greeting. When Week met my eye he jumped, then waved back.

'Mr Week!' called Holmes, and the land agent walked round the bar to us. 'I did not expect to find you here.'

'Nor I you,' said Mr Week. 'I have had a long ride though, and it gives a man a thirst.' The innkeeper set a pint in front of him. 'How is the case going?'

'It is a sad business,' said Holmes, shaking his head. 'I shall have to break the news to Mr Holcombe tonight. If you could be there at dinner, he will need a friend.'

'I've worked for Mr Holcombe these last seven

years, and he knows he can count on me,' said Mr Week. He cast us a look under his brows. 'It is true, then? About the . . .'

'I fear so.'

'Dear me.' Mr Week shook his head in turn, and retired to the corner.

'You are abominably slow with that pint, Watson,' said Holmes, draining his glass. 'I shall have a chat with mine host while you drink up.' He suited the action to the word, and I was treated to the sight of the publican's face frowning, then grinning, a bark of laughter, and the glint of gold as Holmes's hand moved across the bar. Holmes returned shortly afterwards. 'Are you in the mood for a stroll, Watson?'

I gaped at him, but refrained from commenting until we had left the inn and progressed some way down the road. 'What's got into you, Holmes? This morning, with all seriousness, you said you believed in vampires, and now you're cracking jokes in a public house!'

'All will be revealed, Watson.' Holmes sauntered towards the hedge and climbed over a stile. 'I have done what I can for the present; the rest will unwind later. The Holcombes dine at seven, I believe.' And with that I had to be content.

VI

We returned to Mickleton Hall at six that evening, after a thoroughly muddy tramp through the fields. I dreaded to think what the boots would say about our filthy footwear, and applauded my own foresight in bringing spare trousers.

We were approaching our rooms when Mr Holcombe appeared at the end of the corridor. 'Gentlemen, I understand you have news for me.'

'We do,' said Holmes. 'But it is news that cannot be delivered until dinner-time.'

'This is not a game, Mr Holmes.' Holcombe stood firm.

'I know it, Mr Holcombe.' Holmes paused, his hand on the doorknob. 'I have taken the liberty of inviting Dr Maloney to dine with us tonight. I am concerned at the effect of my verdict, and I would be happier in my mind if your physician were present.'

Mr Holcombe's eyes widened, but he nodded, and we gained our rooms without further interference.

Dinner was a sombre affair. All our minds were on the forthcoming revelations. Of all of us, only Mr Week made a good meal; but eventually even he pushed his knife and fork together. Sherlock Holmes waited while the plates were cleared. Then he left the room for a few moments, returned, and stood at the head of the table.

'Dr Watson and I were summoned to Mickleton Hall by an urgent letter from Mr Holcombe, asking us to investigate a case of vampirism. I am no believer in the supernatural, nor in the dark arts, but this case has changed my view.' Holmes turned towards Mr Holcombe. 'Sir, I am afraid that if you were hoping I could find an innocent explanation, you will be disappointed. I am sorry.'

Mr Holcombe bowed his head, then raised it and looked Holmes full in the face. 'I am ready,' he said, simply.

Dr Maloney half rose from his chair. 'Mr Holmes, as a scientist I do not —'

'Dr Maloney, please hear me out, and I think your scientific brain will be satisfied.' The pair locked eyes, and, muttering, the physician sat back down.

'The family presented a tale of a delicate young girl who outgrew her strength, and sadly died. The landlord of the village inn presented a tale of a flighty, vain young miss no better than she should be. Finally, we have the tale of a vampire, the Snow-White Lady, who roams at night and preys on animals — and there are witnesses who will swear to it, and produce victims. They cannot all be true — or can they?'

Holmes returned to his place, picked up his wine glass, and took a sip. 'Yesterday evening, Mr Holcombe, when I looked outside and said I saw nothing — I am afraid I lied. I saw the Snow-White Lady, standing at the edge of your lawn. A young woman all in white, her mouth and hands stained red. I will admit that the sight chilled my blood. If you had asked me at that moment, I would have said I believed in vampires. But I have an advantage over the dark side; my good, level-headed friend Dr Watson, who always sets me right. He gave me a sleeping-draught, as he recommended to you, and I woke in the morning my usual rational, sceptical self.

The next step, obviously, was to inspect your daughter's body, as you had asked Dr Watson to do. We took the precaution of inviting Dr Maloney along, and I am glad we did. Mr Holcombe, are you acquainted with vampire lore?'

Holcombe swallowed, and ran a finger under

his collar. 'I am not,' he muttered. 'I do not believe in such things.'

'Let me enlighten you.' Holmes held his glass to the light, and swirled the blood-red liquid. 'Vampires are supposed to be un-dead, and if they get their fill of blood their bodies are nicely preserved. When we opened the coffin we found the body not decomposed, but as fresh as if Amelia were sleeping. And we also found two little red marks on her neck.'

Mrs Holcombe put her hands to her mouth. 'So Amelia has become a vampire!' she whispered, her eyes huge and terrified.

'No, Mrs Holcombe.' Holmes smiled. 'Again I was set right, this time by the good physician Dr Maloney. "There is no such thing as a vampire", he said. Normally I would agree, but — well, what is a vampire? A parasite which sustains itself by sucking the life-blood from another.' He put the wine glass to his lips, sipped, and set it down on the table. 'I realised that I *was* dealing with a vampire — and the vampire, Mrs Holcombe, is you.'

'Mr Holmes, explain yourself,' thundered Mr Holcombe.

Holmes pointed at Mrs Holcombe. 'Look at her, now she has been found out.'

We looked. All the sweet softness had vanished

from Mrs Holcombe's countenance, and she was almost unrecognisable as the woman we had known. Her dark eyes were hard and opaque as jet, and her mouth formed a scarlet gash in her white face.

Mrs Holcombe sprang up. 'I will not stay and listen to this rubbish. How dare you accuse me!'

A smile played over Holmes's lips, but no mirth showed in it. 'Oh, you will stay, Mrs Holcombe. The servants have my express instructions to let no-one leave this room without my permission. Sit down.'

Her lip curled in a sneer. 'Let's hear it.'

'Amelia was so beautifully arranged,' mused Mr Holmes. 'Like a painting, or a stage set. And those little punctures on her neck —I suspect your sharp little embroidery scissors, Mrs Holcombe — were the final touch. But there is no such thing as a vampire. So how did Mrs Holcombe work this magic? I am afraid it is much more prosaic than a dark lord flying in the night. Amelia did not die from consumption. She was poisoned.'

'Poisoned?' cried Dr Maloney. 'But she was consumptive! I am her physician, and I know!'

'I agree, Dr Maloney. Amelia was consumptive. And when we know someone is very ill, a worsening in their health is almost expected. Now, arsenic preserves a body remarkably. I recall the case of the Styrian arsenic-eaters, whose well-preserved corpses were recognisable years after their burial. Amelia's symptoms — coughing, dizziness, flushed cheeks, cramps and retching — are entirely consistent with arsenic poisoning. First a slow, chronic dose from the beautiful bright green wallpaper — Scheele's green, indeed — riddled with damp in Amelia's room, and the bottle of skin lotion on her dressing table, of a brand containing an unhealthy dose of arsenic. Some fine ladies swear by regular small doses of the poison as a beautifier, and Amelia's pink-and-white complexion and abundant hair attest to its effect. But you were impatient, Mrs Holcombe. I saw the unchanged flypaper in the study, and I wonder if you used the rest of the packet to prepare a lethal dose. I think we will take a sample of Amelia's hair, and make sure of it.'

'How can you accuse me of such things?' wailed Mrs Holcombe, wringing her hands.

'Very easily,' said Holmes, drily. 'I read the spines of the novels on Amelia's bookshelf when I was pretending to examine the window, and found a fine lot of romantic tosh. Exactly the sort of thing to corrupt a young girl and turn her into a flirt at the least. Exactly what a conscientious governess, or a good mother, would not let her read. Add to that the fashion-plates on display, and I suspect you planned to ruin the poor girl's character in the eyes of the neighbourhood, not least in sending her to local events dressed in a way which might be acceptable in London, but seen as nigh on immoral in rural Devonshire.'

'But what of the Snow-White Lady?' Dr Maloney pressed his fingers to his temples. 'Why arrange such a ghastly spectacle?'

'I suspect Mrs Holcombe's eventual aim was to kill her husband, since I presume she is the main beneficiary of her husband's will. Amelia's death was not enough, nor the shameful village gossip about her flighty ways. Therefore Mrs Holcombe set out to produce a sight which would break her husband's heart and, in its horror, cause his death.' Holmes whipped round. 'Ah, you are looking at the curtains, Mrs Holcombe. It is time for the show to begin.'

Holmes walked to the curtains and flung them apart, then opened the doors onto the garden. 'Remember, everyone, there is no such thing as a vampire. Ah, our heroine. I recognise her from last night.'

Before us a white figure stood in the gloom. I could just see the flowing hair and — what was she holding? 'Holmes, she has got hold of a baby!' I cried. 'Stop her!'

‘Don’t worry, Watson, it is in hand.’ Holmes said. We watched, spellbound, as the woman bent her head over the child. When she raised it, her bloodstained lips glistened in the moonlight.

VII

The vampire was so intent on us that she did not see the dark figures creeping up till they were almost on her. We heard a scream, a whooshing sound, and then a wail as one of the men walked forward, dragging a soaked young woman holding a child's doll.

'Got her, sir,' he chuckled. 'Not much of a vampire now, is she?'

'Blast yer,' she growled. 'No job's worth this.' She threw down the doll and tried to wring out her nightgown with her free hand.

Holmes applauded. 'You were wonderful until my accomplices upstaged you, my dear. The blood is extremely convincing from a distance. May I ask — did you bite the dogs and cats, too?'

She giggled. 'Course not! I just pretended, and got a good lot of blood on their fur. Then I put 'em back where I found 'em. Funny sort of practical joke, if you ask me. And this —' She pointed to the doll lying on the grass. 'This is plain creepy.'

'Quite,' said Holmes. 'Do tell me, before you make your exit, which one of our audience hired you.'

The woman wiped her mouth on her white sleeve, leaving a dark-red smear. 'It was her.' And she pointed to the snarling, cornered Mrs Holcombe.

'Thank you,' said Holmes. 'I suggest you go and change out of your wet things, and be more careful about the work you accept in future.'

She snorted, and trudged away over the lawn. While she muttered under her breath, I caught the words 'catch my death of cold', and 'working out in the ruddy sticks' very distinctly.

'I don't understand . . .' Mr Holcombe looked pleadingly at his wife. 'Why would you do such a thing, Mary? What did we ever do to you?'

Mrs Holcombe laughed. I give her the name Mrs Holcombe, but it was as if she had thrown off a skin, and exposed her true nature. 'As the great detective says, Bill, I was impatient. God knows it's dull here, and I deserve a medal for bearing it this long. I tried to get you to move somewhere more exciting, so that I could have some sort of life — but no, the lord of the manor had to stay in his draughty old hall.' She turned to Holmes. 'But you needn't paint me as the lone villain of the piece. It wasn't just me, was it, Matthew?' Her eyes flicked in Mr Week's direction, and he held his hands up as if to ward off the devil.

'She's lying,' he stammered. 'She's trying to pull me into this to save herself. I told her about the situation, but the rest was all her idea.'

'Mr Week, it is no use trying to save your neck. You and Mrs Holcombe were partners in the exaggerated secrecy surrounding our visit. I suspected you almost from the beginning, and when I found you drinking in the public house it was clear where all those nasty rumours had originated. It isn't only Mrs Holcombe who embroiders as a hobby, is it?'

'I don't know what you mean,' muttered Mr Week, his eyes darting about for an escape route.

A chair scraped, and Dr Maloney made his way round the table to whisper in Mr Holcombe's ear. Mr Holcombe shook his head. 'I want to hear it,' he said. 'I want to hear it all.'

'You were an actress, Mrs Holcombe.' Holmes paused. 'I do not think you deserve that name. What is your real name?'

'Find out yourself,' she spat.

'Oh, I shall. If I were within reach of a telegraph-office, I would already know. It was a tiny piece of newsprint which put me on your track. I knew the typeface, but I could not remember where I had seen it before. Then I met with you, and you stood, and sat, and gesticulated, and cried, just as you ought. This time, the landlord of the inn put me right. "Now she *is* a lady," he said. But you are supposed to be a governess who married well, not a fine lady — and not the heroine of a melodrama. It flashed into my head how you hit your mark every time — and I recognised the piece of newsprint as a scrap from *The Stage*. What use would anyone unconnected with the theatre have for that publication? Why would you have it now? *An advertisement*, I thought, *for an actress to play the vampire*, and the Snow-White Lady was unmasked.'

Holmes turned to Mr Week. 'I have not finished with you. I presume you knew this woman beforehand, and helped her to obtain false references when Mr Holcombe sought a governess.'

Mr Week stared straight ahead.

'It will not take me long to discover both your identities,' Holmes said. 'I promise you, you will hang.'

Mrs Holcombe stretched her hands across the table. 'Bill, if ever you loved me —'

Mr Holcombe rose abruptly. 'Do not speak to me again.' He walked over to Holmes and shook his hand. 'Mr Holmes, I am indebted to you. You have saved my life. I will leave you to do what is necessary.' Holmes accompanied him to the door, and after a hushed conversation, we heard the creak of Mr Holcombe's footsteps on the stairs.

'It grows late,' said Holmes. 'I am not sure what hours your local constabulary observe.' His mouth twisted. 'I presume no-one would care for dessert? Very well. In that case I suggest we uphold the regular custom. Gentlemen, we shall remain here while the lady adjourns.'

We gaped at Holmes, who held up a hand, and continued. 'Mrs Holcombe, there is a slight problem with your drawing room, so I have prepared an alternative. I have arranged an escort to your step-daughter's bedroom. Mr Week, as you are no gentleman, you will accompany her. We will enjoy our port and coffee, and perhaps we shall see you later.'

Mrs Holcombe got to her feet. Her eyes flashed, and her mouth was a thin straight line. 'You will burn in hell, Sherlock Holmes!'

'I doubt it,' said Holmes, mildly. 'A little too dramatic for such a small stage, my dear.' The lad in livery took her arm, and marched her to the door.

'Mr Week.' Holmes's eyes glittered. 'You will follow the lady.'

‘I don’t understand.’ Mr Week seemed dazed. ‘Why —’

‘You will see. Dr Watson, would you mind showing Mr Week the way? We wouldn’t want him to get lost.’

I guided the unresisting Mr Week upstairs. The servant stood by the bedroom door. ‘She’s in, sir. I’ll stay here, just in case.’

‘Thank you.’ I opened the door.

The room was as I remembered it — the peeling wallpaper, the bottles on the dressing-table, the novels on the bookshelf. Yet a row of fresh new flypapers hung by the window, and a jug of water and two glasses had been placed on the dressing-table.

Mrs Holcombe was looking out of the window, her back to us.

‘The villagers are still outside,’ I said.

She did not turn around. ‘You haven’t won,’ she said through clenched teeth.

‘Please,’ Mr Week swallowed. ‘Don’t make me go in. I can’t be alone with her.’

‘You’re a coward, Matthew,’ she spat. ‘I always knew it. And as usual, I shall have to do all the work.’ She wheeled round, seized Mr Week’s hand and pulled him into the room. ‘Get out!’ she screamed, and as I backed away she slammed the door in my face.

***

The decanter of port had passed round the table twice when Holmes consulted his watch. 'They have had enough time,' he said. 'I shall see if they are ready to join us. Watson, would you care to accompany me?'

'I shall come too,' said Dr Maloney.

The lad in livery was standing a few feet from the bedroom door. 'Mr Week's not well,' he said, jerking his thumb. 'He's been crying and begging to be set free, but I took no heed, just as you said.'

'Good,' said Holmes. 'And the lady?'

'Nothing. I've heard 'em moving about, and some mighty strange noises, but she hasn't said a word.'

Holmes put his eye to the keyhole. 'Unlock the door, lad, and stand by the stairs.' He waited until the boy had gone before flinging the door open.

We clapped our handkerchiefs to our faces at the stench which met us, and stepped carefully over the pools of waste to the bodies beyond. Mr Week lay face-up, the handles of a pair of small scissors protruding from his neck. A pool of blood was creeping over the rug. His face was dark red and swollen, and his eyes bulged almost from their sockets. Dr Maloney went to him and gently opened his mouth with a finger.

'Asphyxiation,' he said. 'His mouth has been

stuffed with flypaper.'

Mrs Holcombe had arranged herself on the bed, and an empty glass stood on the bedside table. Perhaps she had hoped to present as pretty a picture as her stepdaughter; but her face was covered in scratches, her lips drawn back in a snarl, and her hair matted with vomit.

'The Snow-White Lady is dead.' Holmes said, in a clipped, matter-of-fact voice. 'I should have known from the start.'

'What do you mean?' I asked.

'The first clue was in the letter your friend sent. I do not know if it was Mrs Holcombe or Mr Week who named the vampire, but you will remember the tale of Snow White and her wicked stepmother.'

My eyes strayed to the damp strips of apple-green wallpaper cast onto the floor.

'Precisely,' said Holmes. 'I suggest we call the servants in to deal with this mess. Dr Maloney, will you go to Mr Holcombe and inform him that all is complete.'

'Most certainly,' said Dr Maloney. 'A clear case of death by misadventure.'

VIII

We left Mickleton Hall the next day. I was woken early by the rumble of wheels on gravel, followed by the peal of the door-bell, and peeped outside to see a plain black carriage. I kept to my room until the carriage had left.

We were summoned to a hearty meal in the breakfast room, and I was surprised to find Holcombe there before us, a cup of coffee in front of him, and an unread newspaper by his plate. We exchanged the usual morning pleasantries, and I had barely bitten into a slice of toast when the door-bell pealed again. A maid came to the door. 'Begging pardon, sir, but Mr Jeffers from the village is here, enquiring after you.'

'Tell him I'm not at — no!' Holcombe pulled the napkin from his throat and threw it on the table. 'Show him in.'

The maid bobbed, withdrew, and reappeared shortly afterwards with the publican, holding his hat in both hands as if to protect himself.

'Our Bessie was mopping the front step when she saw the undertaker's cart go by, sir, and we were worried. My boys came back with all sorts of stories last night . . .'

'Sit down, Jeffers. Would you prefer tea, or coffee?'

The publican perched on the extreme edge of a chair, and we watched his face pale, then flush, his fist smack his palm, and his hands cover his mouth, as Mr Holcombe related the particulars of the case. 'I have told you this, Jeffers, so you can put the story straight in the village. My good name, and that of my family, has suffered long enough.'

Jeffers got to his feet, came round the table, and shook Mr Holcombe's hand. 'That I will, sir,' he said, and his voice was hoarse. 'That I will.'

'I shall rent this place, and travel,' said Holcombe, once the door had closed behind Jeffers. 'I am the last of the Holcombes, and I have been shut up here too long. If I had known more of the world —'

'Do not blame yourself,' I said. 'That infernal woman had everyone in her clutches.'

'Perhaps,' said Holcombe, 'but I should have taken better care of my daughter. She will haunt me to my death.' He stood, and shook hands with us both. 'My coachman will be ready whenever you need him. I am going for a walk on the moor.'

We were packed and ready betimes, and found the trap waiting. Our departure from the village of Mickleton was far steadier than our arrival, at the hands of Mr Week.

'Look,' said Holmes as we passed the church.

I looked where he pointed. A group of villagers, Jeffers at the head, were scrubbing the marks from the mausoleum, which was lit by the sharp rays of a fine autumn morning. 'If only all wrongs could be righted so easily,' mused Holmes, as the village vanished behind us.

***

I poked the fire while Holmes huddled in his dressing-gown. 'Your temperature is quite normal, Holmes, and I can detect no symptoms but ill-temper, which as we both know is a chronic condition of yours.'

'Be quiet, Watson, your voice hurts my head. Ring and ask Mrs Hudson for a hot toddy — quietly, mind.' He shivered. 'This is the revenge of that infernal moor. I should never have allowed you to take me on that walk.'

'Have you had your fill of adventure then, Holmes?'

'Watson, even from you that is a remark of surpassing stupidity. Pass my violin, please. I suppose you will request the *Lieder*, since you always do. Your musical diet shows an appalling lack of variety.'

The violin case lay on an occasional table, above which was a mirror, and as I went to fetch it I observed the gleam in Holmes's eyes, and the half-smile curving his lips. I made sure to keep my own expression neutral as I turned with the case in my hand, and settled on the sofa for an afternoon of music.

AFTERWORD AND ACKNOWLEDGEMENTS

I said in the acknowledgements to *A Jar of Thursday* that the ONE Sherlock story I actually planned to write was coming next . . . This one, however, just sort of happened.

Last month I went to a fascinating lecture given by Dr Kathryn Harkup, entitled 'A is for Arsenic: The Poisons of Agatha Christie', which was part of the *Talking Science* series at Daresbury Laboratory. I imagine you can guess where this is leading! The whole talk was excellent, but when the 'Styrian defence' came up, and she suggested that arsenic in corpses might have given rise to vampire legends — well, the lightbulb above my head went PING. I'm currently reading Dr Harkup's book, *A Is For Arsenic*, which is just as much fun as the lecture. I've got as far as Phosphorus.

Many thanks to Julie Eger and Judith Leask,

who read and commented on the story, as did my long-suffering husband Stephen Lenhardt. And of course a round of applause to Sir Arthur Conan Doyle, the original creator.

Finally, thank you for reading *The Case of the Snow-White Lady*. If you would like to leave a short review on Amazon, Goodreads or elsewhere, I'd really appreciate it.

FONT AND IMAGE CREDITS

Fonts: Selfish by Misprinted Type (freeware): http://www.misprintedtype.com/

Balthazar by Dario Manuel Muhafara: https://fonts.google.com/specimen/Balthazar. Licensed under SIL Open Font License, version 1.1: http://scripts.sil.org/OFL

Background photo: Point de Rose by Antjekanje at www.pixabay.com (CC0, image modified)

Cover created using GIMP image editor: www.gimp.org.

ABOUT THE AUTHOR

Liz Hedgecock grew up in London, England, did an English degree, and then took forever to start writing. After several years working in the National Health Service, some short stories crept into the world. A few even won prizes. The stories started to grow longer — and then the murders began…

Liz's reimaginings of Sherlock Holmes, *Bitesize*, a collection of flash fiction, and *Murder At The Playgroup*, a modern cozy mystery, are available in ebook and paperback.

Liz now lives in Cheshire with her husband and two sons, and when she's not writing or child-wrangling you can usually find her reading, messing about on Twitter, or cooing over stuff in museums and art galleries.

OTHER BOOKS BY LIZ HEDGECOCK

Short Stories

The Secret Notebook of Sherlock Holmes
Bitesize

Halloween Sherlock series (novelettes)

The Case of the Snow-White Lady
Sherlock Holmes and the Deathly Fog

Sherlock & Jack series (novellas)

A Jar Of Thursday
Something Blue (autumn 2017)

Mrs Hudson & Sherlock Holmes series (novels)

A House Of Mirrors
In Sherlock's Shadow (autumn 2017)

Pippa Parker Mysteries (novels)

Murder At The Playgroup
Murder In The Choir (2018)

You can also find her here:

http://lizhedgecock.wordpress.com/

http://www.facebook.com/lizhedgecockwrites

http://twitter.com/lizhedgecock

https://www.goodreads.com/lizhedgecock

WHITE
RHINO
BOOKS

26977411R00039

Printed in Great Britain
by Amazon